D0786238

# MY
## SHAPE IS
# SAM

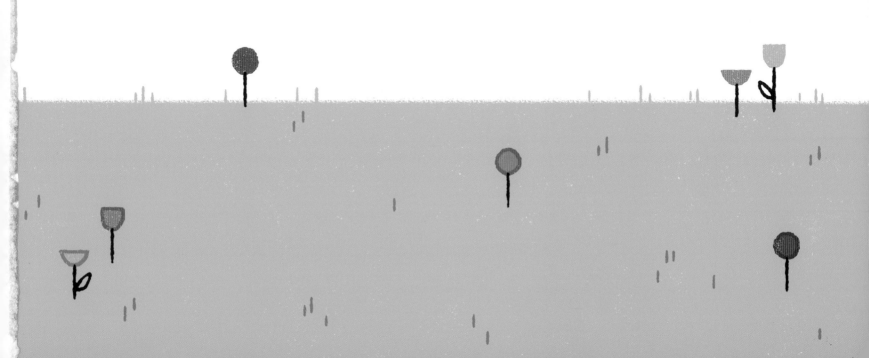

To Thad, for holding me up
and cheering me on.
— A. J.

For my grandma—my BigG—Barbara.
A shape all her own.
— L. N.

Text copyright © 2019 Amanda Jackson. Illustrations copyright © 2019 Lydia Nichols. First published in 2019 by Page Street Kids,
an imprint of Page Street Publishing Co., 27 Congress Street, Suite 105, Salem, MA 01970, www.pagestreetpublishing.com.
All rights reserved. No part of this book may be reproduced or used, in any form or by any means, electronic or mechanical,
without prior permission in writing from the publisher. Distributed by Macmillan, sales in Canada by The Canadian Manda Group.
ISBN-13: 978-1-62414-770-8. ISBN-10: 1-62414-770-4. CIP data for this book is available from the Library of Congress.
This book was typeset in Questrial. The illustrations were done digitally. Printed and bound in Shenzhen, Guangdong, China.
19 20 21 22 23 CCO 5 4 3 2 1

Page Street Publishing uses only materials from suppliers who are committed to responsible and sustainable forest management.
Page Street Publishing protects our planet by donating to nonprofits like The Trustees, which focuses on local land conservation.

trustees

# MY SHAPE IS SAM

Amanda Jackson

illustrated by Lydia Nichols

PAGE STREET KiDS

Sam had four even sides. Four pointy corners.
And like all other squares, he was a builder.

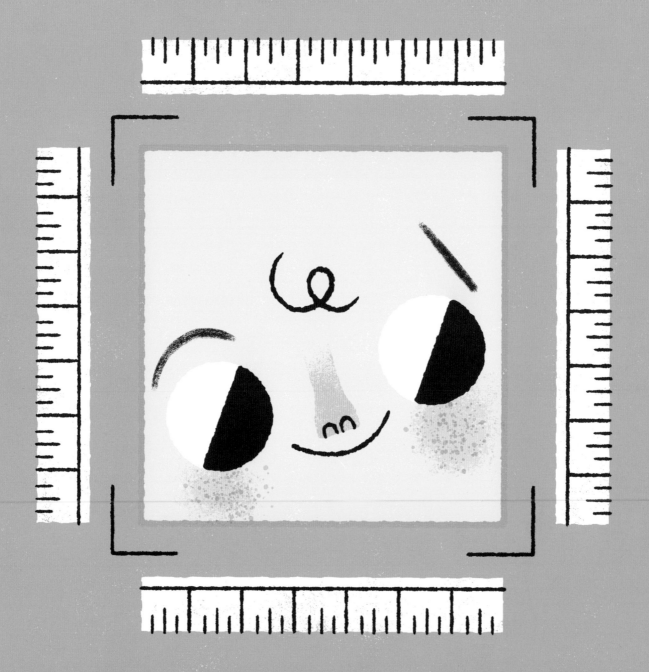

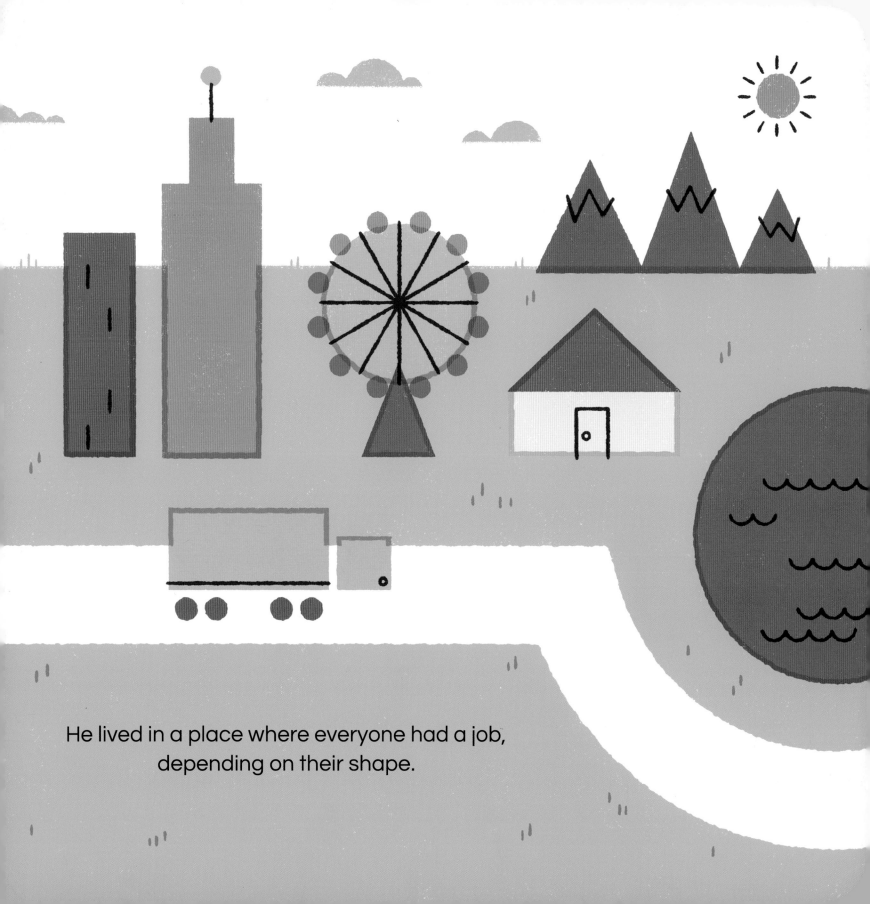

He lived in a place where everyone had a job,
depending on their shape.

Circles were smooth and round.
Good at rolling, spinning, and pushing.
They all turned together to make things go.

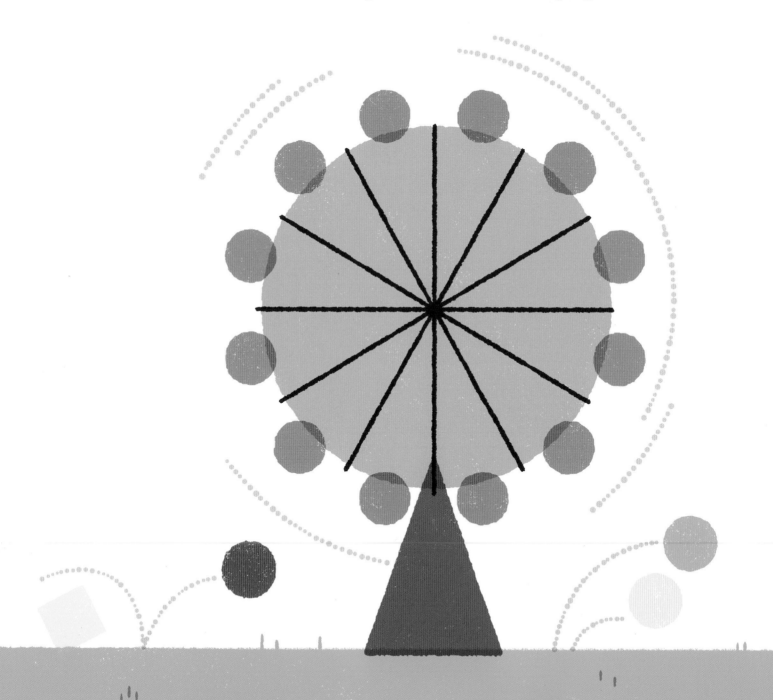

Squares were sturdy and even.
Good at stacking, steadying, and measuring.
They all fit together to make things stay.

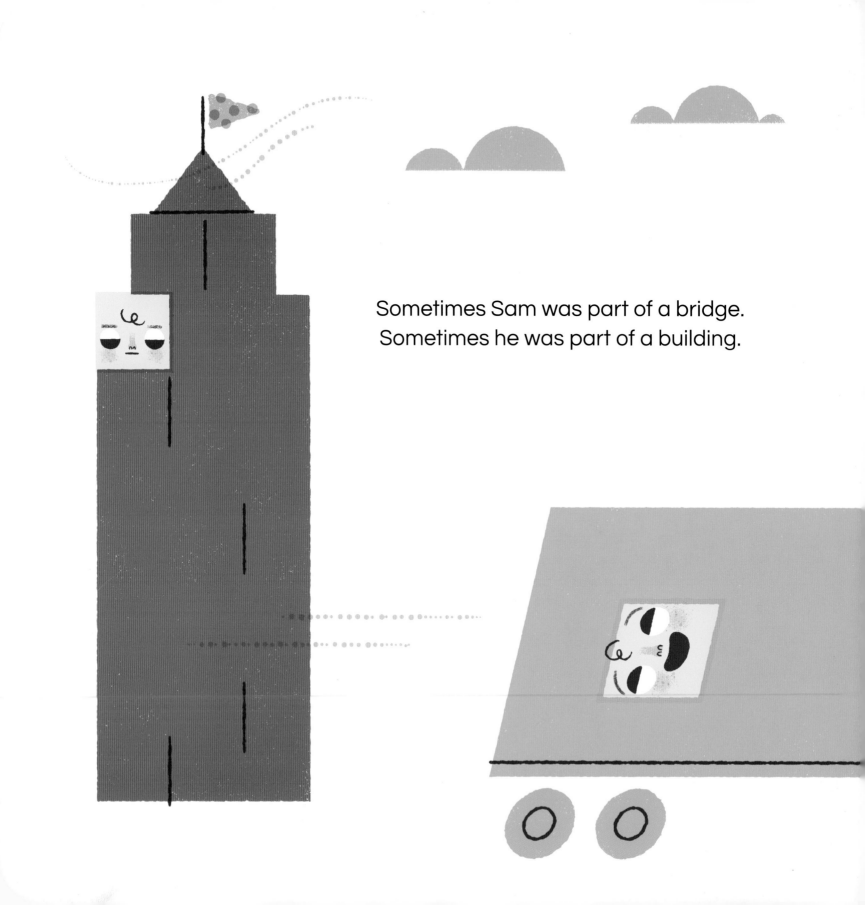

Sometimes Sam was part of a bridge.
Sometimes he was part of a building.

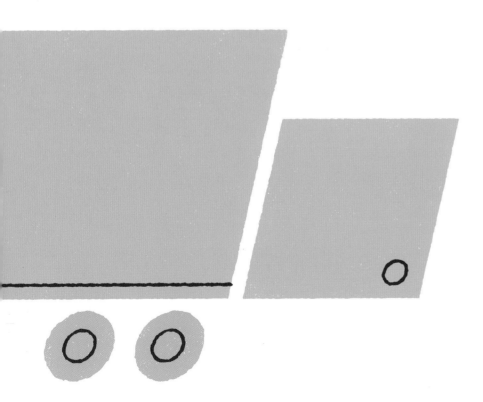

But the best days
were when he was part of
a train rolling over a bridge.
Or a truck zooming past
a building.

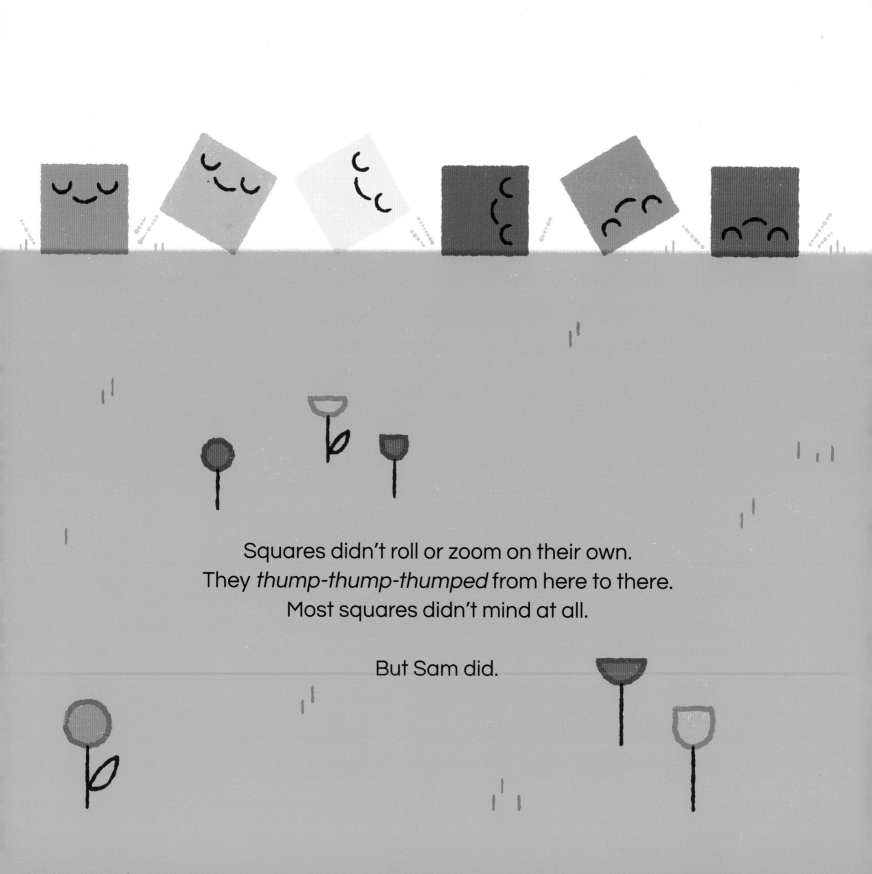

Squares didn't roll or zoom on their own.
They *thump-thump-thumped* from here to there.
Most squares didn't mind at all.

But Sam did.

Sam liked to go fast. Fast was fun.
But mostly, he liked it because that's what circles did.
And even though he had four pointy corners,
Sam didn't really feel like a square.

One day he thumped past a park.
Circles were playing with hoops, racing, and chasing.

Sam got an idea. He found a hoop of his own
and thumped up the hill.

As his last corner left the ground,
he wibbled and wobbled.
Then tipped and tottered . . .
and rolled.

And rolled!

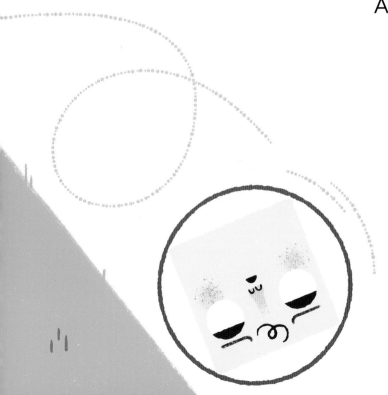

Sam was rolling!
And rolling and YIPPEE and rolling and . . .

CRACK!

His hoop hit a rock,
but Sam just kept rolling with no hoop at all.

Faster and faster he tumbled.
Corner over corner he toppled.
Sam was a whirl of bouncing and

UH-OH

and bopping and . . .

OOF!

He landed with a thud.

The other shapes had never seen
a rolling square before.

"Are you okay?" asked a circle.
"That was AMAZING!" cheered a square.
"Well, I never..." said another square,
shaking her head.

Sam blushed from corner to corner.
He didn't like being watched.
He wanted to go home.

But when he turned to leave,
something inside him nudged,

*Try again.*

Rolling had been wonderful.

*Try again.*

And so he did.

There were bumps.
And bonks.
And a few more thuds.

But it was so much FUN.
Sam felt light as air.

After that day,
he rolled wherever he could.

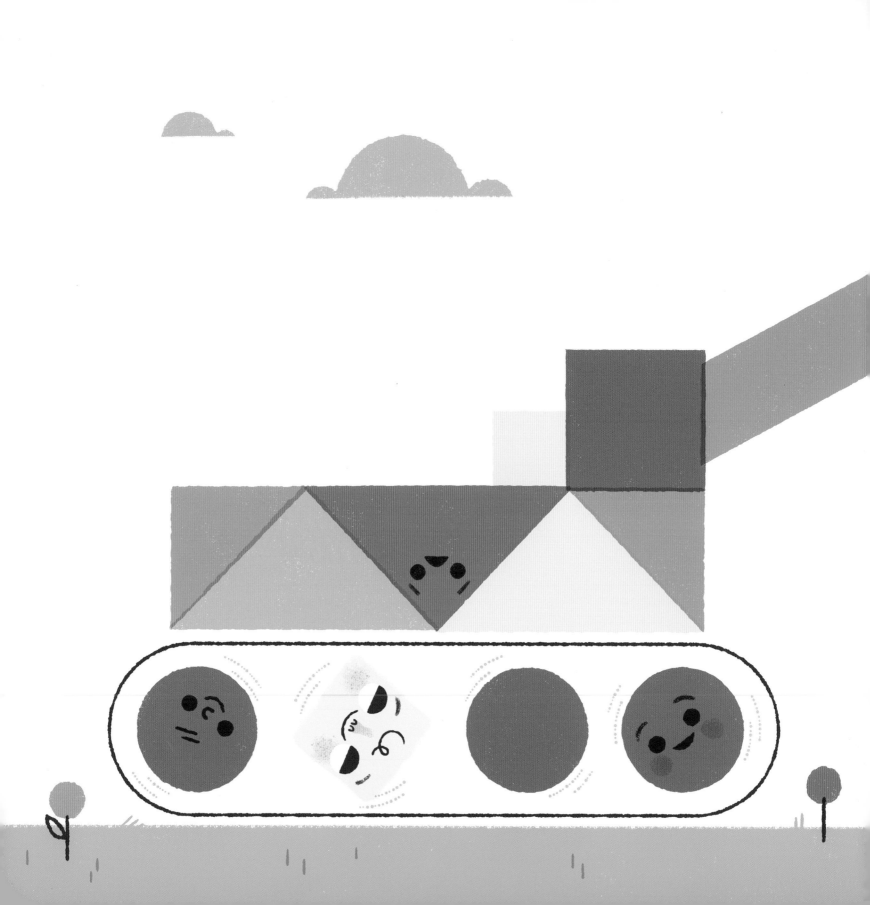

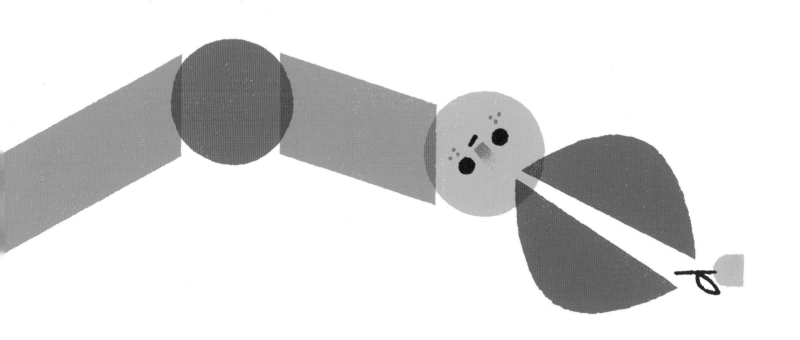

He became so good at rolling,
he got a new job. He wasn't the smoothest,
but the circles welcomed such an
enthusiastic new roller.

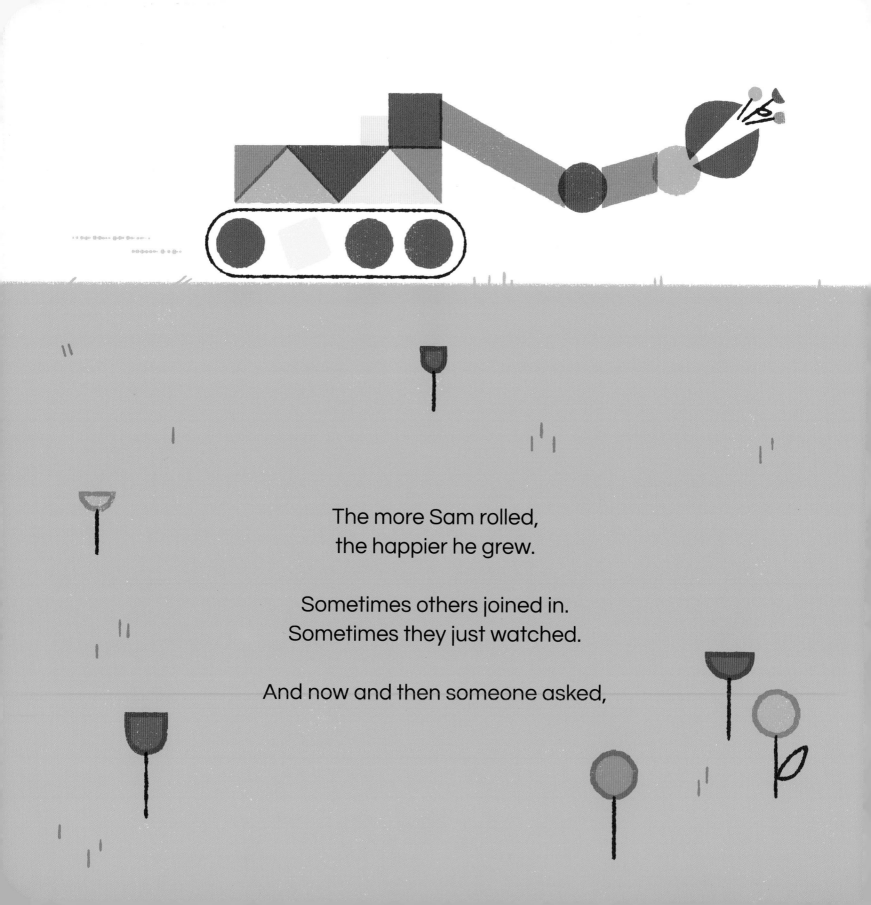

The more Sam rolled,
the happier he grew.

Sometimes others joined in.
Sometimes they just watched.

And now and then someone asked,

"Are you a circle or a square?"

Sam wondered about that too.
He was sturdy like a square,
but he rolled like a circle.

His edges finally felt like his own.

And so he told them,

My shape is Sam!